I Want Another Little
Brother

Poems about Families

Illustrations by
Anna Currey

PUFFIN BOOKS

Acknowledgments

The publishers wish to thank the following for permission to use copyright material:

John Agard, 'Cow Chat' from *No Hickory, No Dickory, No Dock*, Penguin Books, by permission of Caroline Sheldon Literary Agency on behalf of the author, and 'Ask Mummy Ask Daddy' from *I Din Do Nuttin*, Bodley Head, by permission of Random House UK; **Dorothy Aldis**, 'Everybody Says' and 'Little' from *Everything and Anything*, Copyright © 1925-1927, 1953-1955 by Dorothy Aldis, by permission of G P Putnam's Sons, a division of Penguin Putnam Inc; **Valerie Bloom**, 'Water Everywhere', by permission of the author; **John Ciardi**, 'What Someone Said When He Was Spanked On The Day Before His Birthday' from *You Know Who*, 1964, by permission of the Ciardi family; **Heidi Fish**, 'My Folks' from *Cadbury's Ninth Book of Children's Poetry*, 1991, by permission of Cadbury Ltd; **Theresa Heine**, 'Who Is It?', by permission of the author; **Mary Ann Hoberman**, 'Brother', copyright © 1959, renewed 1987 by Mary Ann Hoberman, by permission of Gina Maccoby Literary Agency on behalf of the author and Harcourt Brace & Company; **Michelle Magorian**, 'Babies' from *Orange Paw Marks*, Viking, 1991, p55. Copyright © Michelle Magorian, 1991 by permission of Rogers, Coleridge and White Ltd on behalf of the author; **Colin McNaughton**, 'Potty' from *Who's Been Sleeping in My Porridge*. Copyright © 1990 Colin McNaughton, by permission of Walker Books Ltd; **Lilian Moore**, 'Bedtime Stories' from *See My Lovely Poison Ivy*. Copyright © 1975 by Lilian Moore, by permission of Marian Reiner on behalf of the author; **Judith Nicholls**, 'To the Sea!' from *Wish You Were Here?*, Oxford University Press. Copyright © 1992 by Judith Nicholls, by permission of the author; **Brian Patten**, 'Squeezes' from *Gargling With Jelly*, Penguin Books Ltd. Copyright © Brian Patten 1985, by permission of Rogers, Coleridge and White on behalf of the author; **Vyanne Samuels**, 'Daddy' from *Beams*, Methuen Children's Books, 1990, by permission of Egmont Children's Books; **Carl Saville**, 'Salty Sea' from *Cadbury's Ninth Book of Children's Poetry*, 1991, by permission of Cadbury Ltd; **Charles Thomson**, 'Up to the Ceiling' included in *Mr Mop Has a Floppy Top*, Stanford Books, by permission of the author.

Every effort has been made to trace the copyright holders but if any have been inadvertently overlooked the publishers will be pleased to make the necessary arrangement at the first opportunity.

PUFFIN BOOKS

Published by the Penguin Group

Penguin Putnam Books for Young Readers,

345 Hudson Street, New York, New York 10014, U.S.A.

Penguin Books Ltd, 27 Wrights Lane, London W8 5TZ, England

Penguin Books Australia Ltd, Ringwood, Victoria, Australia

Penguin Books Canada Ltd, 10 Alcorn Avenue, Toronto, Ontario, Canada M4V 3B2

Penguin Books (N.Z.) Ltd, 182-190 Wairau Road, Auckland 10, New Zealand

Penguin Books Ltd, Registered Offices: Harmondsworth, Middlesex, England

First published in Great Britain by Macmillan Children's Books,
a division of Macmillan Publishers Limited, 1999
First published in the United States of America by Puffin Books,
a division of Penguin Putnam Books for Young Readers, 2001

1 3 5 7 9 10 8 6 4 2

This collection copyright © Macmillan Children's Books, 1999
Illustrations copyright © Anna Currey, 1998
All rights reserved

CIP information is available.

Puffin Books ISBN 0-14-056760-7

Printed in Belgium

Contents

Water Everywhere

There's water on the ceiling,
And water on the wall,
There's water in the bedroom,
And water in the hall,
There's water on the landing,
And water on the stair,
Whenever Daddy takes a bath
There's water everywhere.

Valerie Bloom

Up to the Ceiling

Daddy lifts me
up to the ceiling.
Daddy swings me
down to the floor.
Daddy! Daddy!
More! More! MORE!
Up to the ceiling,
down to the floor.

Charles Thomson

My Folks

Dad is the funniest,
Mum is the best,
Lucy is my helper,
and Daniel is a pest.

Heidi Fish (aged 7)

Brother

I had a little brother
And I brought him to my mother
And I said I want another
Little brother for a change.

But she said don't be a bother
So I took him to my father
And I said this little bother
Of a brother's very strange.

But he said one little brother
Is exactly like another
And every little brother
Misbehaves a bit he said.

So I took the little bother
From my mother and my father
And I put the little bother
Of a brother back to bed.

Mary Ann Hoberman

Little Arabella Miller

Little Arabella Miller
Found a woolly caterpillar.
First it crawled upon her mother
Then upon her baby brother.
All said, "Arabella Miller,
Take away that caterpillar!"

Anon.

There was a Little Girl

There was a little girl
Who had a little curl
Right in the middle of her forehead.
When she was good
She was very, very good,
But when she was bad she was horrid.

Henry Wadsworth Longfellow (attrib.)

There was an Old Woman who Lived in a Shoe

There was an old woman
  who lived in a shoe,
She had so many children
  she didn't know what to do;
She gave them some broth
  without any bread;
And whipped them all soundly
  and put them to bed.

Anon.

Ask Mummy Ask Daddy

When I ask Daddy
Daddy says ask Mummy

When I ask Mummy
Mummy says ask Daddy.
I don't know where to go.

Better ask my teddy
he never says no.

John Agard

Daddy

Me so small
And you so tall,
Why can't you get the stars
From the sky after all?

Vyanne Samuels

Mocking Bird

Hush, little baby, don't say a word,
Papa's going to buy you a mocking bird.

If the mocking bird won't sing,
Papa's going to buy you a diamond ring.

If the diamond ring turns to brass,
Papa's going to buy you a looking-glass.

If the looking-glass gets broke,
Papa's going to buy you a billy-goat.

If that billy-goat runs away,
Papa's going to buy you another today.

Anon.

Salty Sea

Salty sandcastle,
Salty sea,
Salty footprints,
Salty me.

Carl Saville (aged 5)

To the Sea!

Who'll be first?
Shoes off,
in a row,
four legs fast,
two legs slow —
Ready now?
Off we go!
Tip-toe,
dip-a-toe,
heel and toe —
Yes or no?
Cold as snow!
All at once,
in we go!
One,
   two,
      three,
         SPLASH!

Judith Nicholls

Squeezes

We love to squeeze bananas,
We love to squeeze ripe plums,
And when they are feeling sad
We love to squeeze our mums.

Brian Patten

Little

I am the sister of him
And he is my brother.
He is too little for us
To talk to each other.

So every morning I show him
My doll and my book;
But every morning he still is
Too little to look.

Dorothy Aldis

What Someone Said When He Was Spanked On the Day Before His Birthday

Some day
I may
Pack my bag and run away.
Some day
I may.
—But not today.

Some night
I might
Slip away in the moonlight.
I might.
Some night.
—But not tonight.

Some night.
Some day.
I might.
I may.
—But right now I think I'll stay.

John Ciardi

Chook, Chook, Chook

Chook, chook, chook, chook, chook,
  Good morning, Mrs Hen.
How many chickens have you got?
  Madam, I've got ten.
Four of them are yellow.
  And four of them are brown,
And two of them are speckled red,
  The nicest in the town.

Anon.

Cow Chat

Mama Moo
Papa Moo
Baby Moo
lying in the grass

Said Mama Moo
to Papa Moo
"When the grass is new
I love to chew"

"And I do too"
said Baby Moo

John Agard

Noise

Billy is blowing his trumpet;
Bertie is banging a tin;
Betty is crying for Mummy
And Bob has pricked Ben with a pin.
Baby is crying out loudly;
He's out on the lawn in his pram.
I am the only one silent
And I've eaten all of the jam.

Anon.

Potty

Don't put that potty on your head, Tim.
Don't put that potty on your head.
  It's not very clean
  And you don't know where it's been,
So don't put that potty on your head.

Colin McNaughton

The Wheels on the Bus

Mime the action of the wheels going round, the mums chattering (you can do this by holding your thumb and four straight fingers to make a beak shape, and opening and closing it), the dads nodding and the kids wriggling.

The wheels on the bus
go round and round,
Round and round,
Round and round,
The wheels on the bus
go round and round,
Over the city streets.

The mums on the bus
go chatter, chatter, chatter,
Chatter, chatter, chatter,
Chatter, chatter, chatter,
The mums on the bus
go chatter, chatter, chatter,
Over the city streets.

The dads on the bus
go nod, nod, nod,
Nod, nod, nod,
Nod, nod, nod,
The dads on the bus
go nod, nod, nod,
Over the city streets.

The kids on the bus
go wriggle, wriggle, wriggle,
Wriggle, wriggle, wriggle,
Wriggle, wriggle, wriggle,
The kids on the bus
go wriggle, wriggle, wriggle,
Over the city streets.

Anon.

Bedtime Stories

"Tell me a story,"
Says Witch's Child.
"About the Beast
So fierce and wild.
About a Ghost
That shrieks and groans
A Skeleton
That rattles bones.
About a Monster
Crawly-creepy.
Something nice
To make me sleepy."

Lilian Moore

Babies

Babies are funny.
They don't speak a lot.
They can't drink from cups
Or sit on a pot.

They like to grip fingers.
They like milk from mummies.
They like having raspberries
Blown on their tummies.

They like being cuddled
And kissed on the head.
But they don't say a lot,
They just dribble instead.

Michelle Magorian

Everybody Says

Everybody says
I look just like my mother.
Everybody says
I'm the image of Aunt Bee.
Everybody says
My nose is like my father's
But *I* want to look like *ME!*

Dorothy Aldis

New Shoes

My shoes are new and squeaky shoes,
They're very shiny, creaky shoes,
I wish I had my leaky shoes
That mother threw away.

I liked my old, brown, leaky shoes
Much better than these creaky shoes,
These shiny, creaky, squeaky shoes
I've got to wear today.

Anon.

Who Is It?

Take . . .
   A head, some shoulders, knees, and toes,
   A mouth and eyes that see,
   A pair of legs, two feet, one nose,
   And what you've got is

                      ME!

Theresa Heine

Flowers Grow Like This

Flowers grow like this,

Cup your hands.

Trees grow like this;

Spread your arms out wide.

I grow
Just like that!

Jump up and stretch.

Anon.